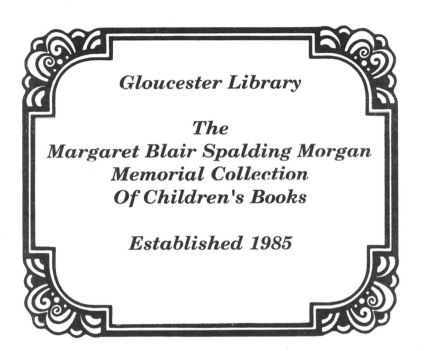

BEYOND THE GRAVE

An Up2U Mystery Adventure

magic wagon

By: Dotti Enderle
Illustrated by: Mary Uhles

visit us at www.abdopublishing.com

Printed in the United States of America, North Mankato, Minnesota.
052013
092013
 This book contains at least 10% recycled materials.

Written by Dotti Enderle
Illustrated by Mary Uhles
Edited by Stephanie Hedlund and Megan Gunderson
Cover and interior design by Neil Klinepier

Library of Congress Cataloging-in-Publication Data

Enderle, Dotti, 1954-
   Beyond the grave : an Up2U mystery adventure / by Dotti Enderle ;
illustrated by Mary Uhles.
       p. cm. -- (Up2U adventures)
   Summary: Dylan's hobby is getting interesting gravestone rubbings
from the old cemetery, and he thinks that one from Dr. Naper,
Cedarville's own Dr. Frankenstein, would be the perfect addition to
his class history project--so which of three possible endings will you
choose for Dylan?
   ISBN 978-1-61641-964-6
1. Plot-your-own stories. 2. Haunted cemeteries--Juvenile fiction.
3. Hobbies--Juvenile fiction. 4. Rubbing--Juvenile fiction. 5. Horror
tales. [1. Haunted places--Fiction. 2. Hobbies--Fiction. 3. Horror
stories. 4. Plot-your-own stories.] I. Uhles, Mary, 1972- ill. II. Title.
   PZ7.E69645Bf 2013
     813.6--dc23
                                    2013001074

TABLE OF CONTENTS

A CREEPY HOBBY

"I'm not going in there," Michael said, peering through the doorway. "Your room creeps me out." He had the look of someone entering a House of Horrors.

Dylan rolled his eyes. "Quit being such a baby. Nothing in here will bite you."

"I'm not so sure." Michael inched in a teeny bit, but he stayed close to the door.

"Seriously, dude," Dylan said, "we can't do this homework if you're standing out in the hall." Why did Mrs. Tottenham have to pick the biggest wimp in class to team with him on the history project?

Michael grimaced. "Why can't we do it in your living room?"

"Because my mom has the TV blaring. And trust me, she's not going to turn off Dr. Phil. "

Michael shuffled all the way in and dropped his backpack to the floor. He nodded toward Dylan's posters and said, "How can you even sleep in here? It looks like a graveyard."

Dylan took that as a compliment. All of his posters contained epitaphs of people long dead. "They're just grave rubbings."

"Of tombstones," Michael countered.

"So what? It's my hobby."

"A creepy hobby," Michael said, rubbing his arms like someone scrubbing away goose bumps.

"You have to admit, some of these are pretty great." Dylan pointed out a few.

Here Lies the Body of Theodore Wake
Instead of His Whip, He Picked Up a Snake
1833 – 1891

Harriet Honey
Too Sweet to Die So Young
1867 – 1887

Peter Durbin
His Hiccups Are Cured at Last
1784 – 1848

"How do you do it?" Michael asked.

Dylan shrugged. "It's easy. I just tape some paper to a headstone and rub it with a charcoal stick."

"No, I mean . . . aren't you scared?"

Dylan threw back his head and laughed. "Scared of what? They're dead, Michael. These words are all they have left. I don't think they mind me borrowing them. And besides, they should be honored. I put a lot of time and work into these posters. Here's my latest."

He nodded toward a rubbing tacked near the window. "I got it last Friday."

Abel Cain
1809 – 1872
A Brother to Us All

"Okay, I admit they are pretty funny," Michael said. "I never see epitaphs like that where my grandpa is buried."

"That's because he's buried in the Cedarville Cemetery. Those headstones are boring. I do my grave rubbings in the old Sleep Haven graveyard by the highway."

"I've got to hand it to you, man, you're brave. The dead scare me."

Dylan sat tall. "None of the dead in that cemetery scare me. But there's a living person there who makes my toes curl."

Michael's eyebrows rose. "Who?"

"Digger O'Malley, the cemetery caretaker. That old goat hates me. He's worried I'll damage the headstones. He's run me off a few times. And the last time he held his shovel to my chin and cursed."

Just thinking about Digger's glaring eyes made pinpricks dance up Dylan's spine. Then, doing his best Digger impersonation, he said, "These headstones are old and frail. You keep rubbing on them and they'll crumble like stale biscuits."

Michael blinked. "Why do you keep going back?" he asked.

"I told you—it's my hobby."

"But isn't it illegal to go into a cemetery at night?" Michael asked.

Dylan grinned. "It's no big deal if you don't get caught."

"If it's something you can get caught at, it's a big deal!" Michael argued.

Dylan glanced at his watch. "Right now the big deal is getting this project done. Who are we going to do our report on?"

Michael gulped. "No one scary, I hope."

EARTH TO DYLAN

Michael unzipped his backpack and pulled out the assignment sheet. "Here is the assignment." He passed it over to Dylan so they could look it over together. It read:

1. Your subject must be a historical figure from Cedarville.

2. How did this person make an impact?

3. Did this person make an impact outside our town as well?

4. What impressed you most about this person?

5. Create a poster, diorama, or timeline. Use visual aids when possible.

6. *Sources must include books and articles. Do not rely on Web sites for all your research!*

"Blah. Historical figures are so boring," Dylan droned. "They ride into town, stub a toe, and a statue is constructed in their honor."

"Not all historical figures are boring," Michael said.

"The ones in Cedarville are." Dylan grabbed his laptop. "What have any of them done besides build a gigantic cheese grater?"

It was true. Cedarville was known for having the World's Largest Cheese Grater. Every year the town holds its annual Cheesy Festival. People bring all types of cheeses to grate— Swiss cheese, cheddar cheese, goat cheese, and Gouda. Due to its armpit smell, Limburger is no longer allowed. The three-day festival provides a mountain of nachos, barrels of mac and cheese, and a truckload of grilled cheese sandwiches. Tourists love it!

"Uh . . ." Michael twitched his mouth, thinking.

"We need to find someone who is famous, but not so famous," Dylan said. "Not someone the whole class is going to be writing about." He opened a search engine and typed *Cedarville historical figures*. Several popped up, including Bob Ratner, the man who'd built the World's Largest Cheese Grater.

Michael tapped the screen. "How about this guy, Jacob Doolittle?"

Dylan squinted at the screen. "Who's he?"

"He brought the railroad to Cedarville."

"No way," Dylan said, shaking his head. "Thanks to him, every time we're late for the movies it's because we're stuck at the train crossing."

"Yeah," Michael agreed, "and the earlier you leave, the longer the train."

They went back to scanning the Cedarville Web site. Michael pointed out another name. "We could do one on Roberta Roberts. She created the first map of Cedarville. Not many women were mapmakers in those days."

Dylan brushed his hair out of his eyes. "Are you kidding? Every girl in class will be doing a report on her. Besides, we have GPS now." He continued scrolling the list.

"Hey," Michael said, "how about Daniel 'Scoop' Davidson?"

"Who?" Dylan asked.

"This dude." Michael jabbed his finger on the name.

They read Scoop's biography.

Daniel Davidson, reporter for the Cedarville Post, *earned the nickname "Scoop" because of his ability to scoop up the best news stories. He was the first to discover that Mayor Winkleman was skimming cash from the town's treasury. He helped nab Mildred Gable for hiding the neighbors' pets and returning them for a reward. And he caught Dewey Downton, the underwear thief. But he was most famous for uncovering the monstrous secrets of Dr. Thaddeus Naper, who came to be known as Cedarville's Frankenstein.*

Michael's eyes lit. "A report on a reporter. How great is that?"

But Dylan's mind was cranking. "Cedarville's Frankenstein," he whispered.

"Yeah," Michael said. "Scoop must've been one great newsman. He's perfect for our assignment."

"Dr. Thaddeus Naper," Dylan muttered.

Michael snapped his fingers in front of Dylan. "Hey, Earth to Dylan."

Dylan smiled. "This is perfect."

"I know, right?" Michael agreed. "Scoop's our man."

"No, not Scoop," Dylan said, tapping his fingertips together. "We're doing our report on the evil doctor."

DR. THADDEUS NAPER

Michael's face turned as white as his teeth. "He's not a historical figure."

"Sure he is," Dylan said. "He lived here. He died here. He got his name in the paper. I think that qualifies."

"But he didn't do anything heroic," Michael protested.

Dylan picked up the assignment sheet and waved it in Michael's face. "Mrs. Tottenham didn't say it had to be a hero. She just said it had to be a historical figure."

Dylan quickly typed *Dr. Thaddeus Naper* into the search engine.

Thaddeus Naper, MD, practiced medicine in Cedarville from 1875 to 1912. He earned the nickname "Cedarville's Frankenstein" because of the vile experiments he conducted in his clinic basement. Dr. Naper kept body parts from all his surgeries to create a living monster. His wicked plans were uncovered by Daniel "Scoop" Davidson, reporter for the Cedarville Post.

Scoop became suspicious after noticing that Dr. Naper had installed four lightning rods on the clinic roof. Going undercover, Scoop sneaked into the basement where he found the pieced-together body of a creature. The monster's head was wired to the lightning rods. Luckily, Cedarville was suffering from a drought that year and no storms were forecast.

During his trial, Dr. Naper told the jury that the monster was created to scare off the tourists. Because of the location of the

World's Largest Cheese Grater, they blocked the street between his home and the clinic.

Dr. Naper was committed to the Cedarville Asylum for the Insane. He died two years later and was laid to rest in the Sleep Haven Cemetery.

Dylan practically jumped for joy. "He's perfect!"

"Perfect?" Michael asked, looking pale.

"Can you think of anyone better?" Dylan asked.

Michael chewed is pinky nail. "Uh . . . I bet *all* the girls aren't doing reports on Roberta, the mapmaker. She seems like the clear choice."

Dylan thumped the computer screen. "Michael, this is A+ material."

"Can we please do our report on a subject that won't give me nightmares?" Michael asked, his eyes pleading.

Dylan huffed. "I'm counting on your help, okay? We'll swing by the library for some more info, then we'll make a poster."

Of course, he didn't dare tell Michael his ultimate plan. If Dr. Naper was buried in the Sleep Haven Cemetery, a grave rubbing of his headstone would be the perfect visual aid.

SCOOP'S SCOOP

Dylan pushed through the library doors and headed straight to the information desk. Michael followed along.

"We're looking for some information on one of our town's historical figures," Dylan said, grinning innocently.

The woman behind the desk—whose name tag said Joyce—crinkled her nose and pointed to a table full of Dylan's classmates. "You and everyone else."

Dylan noticed they were all girls. "But we don't want info on Roberta Roberts. Maps are so boring."

Joyce crinkled her nose again. "So what exactly are you looking for?"

Dylan's smile brightened. "We're looking for a monster. Have you ever heard of Dr. Thaddeus Naper?"

She did another nose twitch. "No, but I'll see what I can find."

Minutes later, Joyce dumped two books, four magazines, and nearly a year's worth of old newspapers on a table near the wall. She crinkled her nose and blinked. "This is all I could find."

"Thanks," Dylan said as he and Michael pulled up their chairs.

Dylan shuffled though the heap and held up the two books, *The History of Cedarville* and *Cedarville—There Is No "Grater" Town*. Both had been written on an ancient typewriter and bound by rusty staples. Dylan thumbed through the second one. There were lots of old-timey photos inside. One was of Cedarville in the early 1900s. Back then the town was just a long row of squatty buildings that reminded Dylan of a Lego village. On the street corner was a cockeyed building of brown brick with the words *Cedarville Medical* etched into the wall.

There were plenty of drawings and pictures of historical figures, including a speckled photograph of Scoop Davidson. Scoop stood in a doorway, grinning, while holding a large boxy camera with an accordion lens. There wasn't much information about him, and none about the fiend he'd discovered. Were the townspeople trying to hide something?

Dylan and Michael thumbed through the magazines. They were mostly filled with farm reports, town gossip, and cheese recipes. Nothing useful for their assignment.

Dylan eyed the yellowed copies of the *Cedarville Post. Sigh.* This could take a while. But the first one he picked up—June 11, 1912—

had an article called "Lightning Never Strikes" by Daniel Davidson.

Dylan straightened in his chair and whispered, "I found something."

Michael moved next to Dylan and they read:

Four lightning rods. No one has four lightning rods. Especially on a building as small as the Cedarville Medical Center. I had to get to the bottom of this.

I made an appointment with Dr. Naper, claiming to have a bad case of hives. On the day of my visit, I wore my gray tweed suit, which always chafes my skin and gives me a rash. The doctor never suspected a thing.

While Dr. Naper mixed up some vile-smelling cream, I engaged him in conversation. "Why four lightning rods?" I asked.

His face grew as pale as the cream. I knew then he had something to hide.

"One can never be too careful," he replied.

He added some foul powder to the cream and blended it with his index finger, leering as he stirred.

"But four lightning rods?" I pursued.

He glared at me, then set the cream down. Retrieving a huge syringe with a pencil-sized needle, he said, "Perhaps an injection would work faster than the cream."

I panicked as he approached. What was in that syringe?

But fortune was on my side. The door flew open and the nurse burst in. She informed the doctor that a tourist was waiting in the emergency room. He had cut himself on the town's cheese grater and was bleeding badly. The doctor sneered and stormed out.

Seeing my chance, I slipped out the back door, retrieved my camera from my car, then snuck back in. I carefully crept down a narrow hall to the basement door. I had a feeling that the lightning rods were attached to whatever was in the basement.

Using my pocket knife, I picked the lock and quietly tiptoed down the dark staircase. The room was dank and clammy and smelled like a moldy shower curtain. I found a candle and lit it. Then what I saw nearly stopped my heart!

Lying on a metal table was a most hideous creature. His feet were the size of apple crates. His hands were like oven mitts. And his oblong head was stitched together from eyebrows to chin. Needles and tubes poked out of his arms, and metal wires were connected to his ears. I knew immediately that the wires were attached to the lightning rods on the roof.

The doctor's plan suddenly became clear. He intended to create a living monster just like the one in Mary Shelley's novel Frankenstein.

It was then that I heard shuffling behind me. I turned to see Dr. Naper holding the syringe high above my head, ready to plunge it into my neck. His eyes were wild.

"So you've found Monty," he said, referring to his monster. Yes, he had already named it like a pet.

I thought fast. Lifting my camera I yelled, "Say cheese!" Then I snapped a picture, blinding him with the flash. I raced out of the basement, locked the door, then hurried two blocks away to the police station where I immediately reported my findings.

Dr. Naper was arrested and sent to the Cedarville Asylum for the Insane. Monty was buried in an unknown grave.

Below the article was a grainy photo, taken
by the brave Scoop Davidson.

DON'T PANIC

"This is incredible!" Dylan cried.

Michael stared at the photos, looking like he might puke. Dylan nudged him.

"This is definitely A+ material," Dylan announced. He was now excited for this research project.

Michael snapped out of his daze. "I may never get that image out of my head," he muttered.

As usual, Dylan ignored him. "With these photos and a grave rubbing of the doctor's headstone, we'll have the best report in the class."

Michael scooted back, glaring. "Who said anything about a grave rubbing?"

Oops! "You have to admit," Dylan defended, "a poster of the epitaph would go great with the report."

"Okay," Michael said. "You do the grave rubbing while I get photocopies of these pictures, then I can—"

Dylan held up his hand, stopping Michael before he could complete the sentence. "We're not going to split up the assignment. We'll do it together, as a team."

Michael's face turned three shades lighter. "B-but . . . I . . ."

Dylan smiled. "Don't panic. It's easy."

"Yeah? What about the caretaker? Won't he throw us out?"

"Don't worry," Dylan assured him. "I know a great way to avoid him."

Michael raised his eyebrows, waiting for the great way to be revealed.

Dylan leaned in and whispered, "We go at night. I figure by then Digger will be off in his cave somewhere, hibernating."

Though it seemed impossible, Michael turned even whiter. "At night? No way!"

"Michael, do you want this A+ or not?"

"Not if it means going to a graveyard after dark," Michael whined.

Dylan grinned. "We'll meet tomorrow night.

"B-b-but . . .," Michael stammered.

Dylan patted him on the back. "It'll be fun."

* * *

Dylan spent the afternoon getting ready. He went to the Sleepy Haven Web site and downloaded a map of the cemetery. Each grave was linked by a number. He ran his finger down the list of names.

56. John Karmen

57. Elizabeth Grayson

58. Dr. Thaddeus Naper.

There. Dylan moved his finger across, searching for grave number fifty-eight. It was marked next to the drawing of the Hanging Tree—a massive oak near the center of the graveyard. Long ago, condemned criminals were hanged from that tree. And even though there hasn't been a hanging in nearly a century, it still has that sinister name.

Now that Dylan knew where to find the grave, he filled his backpack for the break-in. He packed charcoal, art paper, duct tape, a flashlight, and his camera. Especially his camera. Of all his grave rubbings, this would be his prize. He'd get Michael to snap a picture of him holding it up proudly.

He stretched back on his bed, looking at the other rubbings on his wall. He had so many, and yet he'd trade them all for just one. The one he'd create tomorrow night.

Dylan closed his eyes and smiled. *Beware Dr. Naper . . . I'm coming for you.*

A NIGHT IN THE CEMETERY

The pink sky had grown black when Dylan and Michael finally reached the graveyard. They hid their bikes behind some bushes, checking that no one driving down the highway could see them. Then they approached the rusty old gate. Its loopy iron bars reminded Dylan of an angel's harp. A beady-eyed crow sat perched on top of it. *Caw! Caw!* Was it an omen of bad luck?

"See anyone?" he asked Michael as he scanned the area.

Michael shook his head. He'd gone so pale he practically glowed in the dark.

Dylan tugged at the heavy gate. It didn't budge. "Locked! I knew this wouldn't be easy."

Michael sighed. "Looks like we'll have to go home and make our own poster. We already have those cool pictures and I bet we can find more online—"

"We're not going back," Dylan interrupted.

Michael slumped. "But we can't get in."

Dylan rattled the gate again. "I'm not leaving without that epitaph."

Then he was on the move.

"Wait," Michael whispered, scurrying after him.

Dylan ran his hand along the rock wall that surrounded the cemetery. He examined each stone.

Michael crept close. "Dylan, this has disaster written all over it."

"It'll only be a disaster if you blow it. Now come on."

"But what if we get caught?"

"We won't," Dylan said. He wound around to the side, then grinned. "Here's our way in." He'd found a caved-in portion of the wall with a small mound of rocks lying in a heap at the bottom. "Dr. Naper, here I come."

Dylan pitched his backpack over, stepped onto the rocks, and hoisted himself up to the top of the wall. He flattened against it and quickly scanned the area below.

"Do you see anyone, or . . . or . . . anything?" Michael asked, his voice trembling.

"Shhhhhh!" Dylan shifted and looked back. "Keep it down. I don't want to get kicked out before we even get in. We've got to keep an eye out for Digger and his grungy shovel."

Michael stared up. "I thought you said he wouldn't be here at night?"

"He shouldn't be, but the guy's got a built-in radar or something. If he's anywhere around, he'll find us."

"This is getting riskier by the minute," Michael whined.

Dylan ignored him. Seeing that the coast was clear, he swung his legs around, hung for a moment on the other side of the wall, then let go. He dropped about six feet to the ground. He froze, listening for any unusual sounds. All he heard was a chorus of crickets, led by an owl somewhere in a distant tree.

Dylan picked up his backpack and slung it over his shoulder. "Come on," he told Michael.

Michael scrambled up the wall, grunting and panting and kicking loose rocks. "This isn't easy," he huffed.

"Stop complaining and come on."

Michael tumbled off the wall to the bottom of the other side. "Oomph!" He brushed the dirt from the seat of his pants. "We better get an A for this."

"We'll get an A+," Dylan assured him. He pointed toward the middle of the cemetery. "The crazy doctor's buried way over there, near the Hanging Tree." It towered over the other trees—its limbs gnarled and twisted like a crazy old hunchback.

"The what?" Michael asked.

"The Hanging Tree—it's that old tree up ahead where they hanged criminals years ago."

Michael looked like he might puke. "Oh great. Now there are criminals and hangings? Couldn't you have told me this before? A B- is starting to sound pretty good. At least we would live to earn it."

"Come on," Dylan said.

Michael made an exceptionally loud gulping sound as he followed.

CAUGHT RED-HANDED

Dylan had gone in the cemetery during the day, but he'd never been at night. The tombstones jutted up like crooked teeth and their shadows fell like toppled dominoes. And why did it smell like a wet towel? He ran his hand through his hair as they lurked forward.

Dry leaves snapped under their shoes. A chill trickled down Dylan's neck. *Wait, are we being followed?* he wondered. He stopped and looked back.

"What?" Michael asked, clearly shaking from head to sneakers.

"Nothing." Dylan licked his lips. "Just darkness. Let's hurry." Should he admit to

Michael that he was starting to get a little freaked out, too?

Michael moved a bit closer. "Uh . . . Dylan. I have to use the bathroom."

"Just hang on."

"I don't know if I can."

"You can," Dylan said.

They wound their way through a maze of headstones, mausoleums, and angelic statues. The Hanging Tree was just ahead.

"Hurry," Dylan urged, breaking into a sprint.

"Wait up," Michael called softly.

Dylan didn't wait. He wanted that grave rubbing badly. He wandered over to the area where Naper should be buried.

Michael caught up to him, panting. While Dylan was checking out the headstones, Michael was checking out the tree.

"How many people do you think they hanged here?"

Dylan shrugged. "Who knows," he replied. "This town was probably full of thieves and murderers back then. I'm sure they deserved it."

Michael gulped again.

Then Dylan found it. "There." They rushed over to the sagging headstone. The epitaph read:

Doctor Thaddeus Naper
1846 – 1914
Here Lies the Real Monster

Dylan rubbed his palms together in excitement. "This is great."

"The words are sort of worn down," Michael said. "Will you be able to do this?"

Dylan squatted next to it and ran his hand down the cold stone. "What doesn't show up on the paper, I'll fill in later. Are you ready?"

"I'm ready to leave," Michael answered. "And I still need to use the bathroom."

Dylan grinned. "Trust me, this won't take long. I'm a pro."

He quickly unzipped his backpack, cutting into the quiet and scaring away two large crows. They flapped and cawed as they flitted from a limb of the Hanging Tree.

The boys froze.

"Could you be any louder?" Michael whispered.

"Sorry," Dylan said, removing the flashlight and handing it to Michael. He tried removing the paper as quietly as possible, but it crackled and snapped like popcorn in a microwave.

Michael gave him an anxious look.

Dylan smiled. "Yeah, I know. I'm making enough noise to wake the dead."

"Not funny," Michael spouted.

But grave rubbing is a noisy hobby. When Dylan tore the duct tape it echoed like a small explosion. He reached into his backpack again and dug out several fat charcoal sticks. "Watch and learn."

Just then the flashlight flickered, blinking on and off. Michael tapped it with the heel of his hand. "Oh great. Did you pack extra batteries?"

"Don't need 'em," Dylan said, brushing back his hair. "I can do this blindfolded."

Michael dropped the flashlight back into the backpack. "I'd feel better if you could see what you're doing. Remember . . . A+."

"I've got this," Dylan assured him. Turning the charcoal to its side, he circled it round and round against the paper. But now he wished they'd come a little earlier. This would be so much easier if there were a full moon. He glanced up. The sky was as black as ink.

Words formed on the paper, but it was just too dark to make them out. He really hoped he was getting all the details. Of course he wouldn't say that to Michael. Not after all the bragging.

Rubbing a little harder and faster, he moved the charcoal like he was wiping a windshield. After a couple of minutes, he heard the crackling of leaves again.

"Chill out, Michael. I'm almost done," Dylan said. That wasn't exactly the truth. He still had half of the poster left to fill in, but he needed Michael to say calm.

Silence followed.

"Michael?"

The pointed end of a shovel dropped down like a spear, shattering one of the charcoal sticks laying in the dirt.

Digger O'Malley glared down at Dylan. "How many times do I have to throw you out of here?"

"I . . . uh . . . ," Dylan stuttered.

"I've told you over and over to stop rubbing on my tombstones!"

Dylan cowered, shivering like a wet dog. "It's for a school project."

Digger leaned in close, gripping the shovel's handle. His breath smelled like a clogged toilet. "Since when do teachers assign this monkey business for homework?"

"It really is for school," Dylan said. Where'd that coward Michael go?

Digger's yellow eyes burned into him. "I don't care about that. I only care about these graves. You kids have no respect." Digger glanced at the paper taped to the headstone. "Now gather up your stuff and get out."

"Uh . . . yes, sir."

"And remember, next time I'll call the cops." He plucked his shovel out of the dirt and dragged it behind him as he lumbered away.

Phew! Dylan deflated like a balloon. He'd promised to leave, but he couldn't rush off and leave the grave rubbing undone. Not this one. If he worked fast, it'd only take a minute to finish it. Digger wouldn't know the difference . . .

THE ENDING IS Up2U!

If you think Dylan meets Dr. Naper, keep reading on page 51.

If you think Dylan takes a grave rubbing of his own gravestone, go to page 63.

But if you want Dylan to face off against all of the ghosts of his grave rubbings, go to page 71.

ENDING 1: CAUGHT!

Dylan worked like crazy, rubbing the charcoal against the paper. "A+ . . . A+ . . . ," he repeated over and over.

The graveyard had filled with fog and spooky sounds. He heard creaking branches, katydids, and a howling dog.

I'm not leaving until I get this grave rubbing!

Someone stepped up behind him. Finally!

"Michael, where have you be—" As he turned, the words caught in his throat. His mouth plopped open and the charcoal slipped from his hand. "Uh . . . uh . . ."

"Not who you were expecting?" Dr. Thaddeus Naper asked.

Dylan trembled as he stared up at the ragged ghost.

"I was just—" Dylan started.

The doctor grinned, flashing his phantom yellow teeth. "I know what you were doing. You were stealing my epitaph." His cold breath rolled like smoke through the soupy haze. It smelled like fried chicken left in the bucket to rot.

"Ahhhh!" Dylan shot back, slamming against the headstone. "I wasn't stealing it. I was just copying it. There's a difference."

The doctor knelt in front of him. "Do you see how worn it is? If everyone copied it, I'd fade away into nothingness. People would stroll by, look at my headstone, and think, "Hmmm, I wonder who is buried there."

Dylan's mind whirled as his heart pounded. "Michael! Michael!"

Naper's cackle was like acid, burning into Dylan ears. "Your friend was smart. He deserted you a while back."

Dylan squirmed. "Digger, help!"

"He's gone for the night," the doctor said. "He's no use either."

"Just let me go," Dylan begged. "I promise to tear this grave rubbing up and never come back again."

"What? You were so eager to steal it, and now you want to rip it apart? Do you think so little of it now?" Naper asked.

Dylan sniffled, fighting tears. "Please don't hurt me."

"I won't hurt you. I'd never hurt anyone."

Dylan sighed with relief.

"But Monty will." The doctor pointed a skeletal finger toward the Hanging Tree.

Dylan gasped. A monstrous creature the size of a grizzly came lumbering forward. He looked just like he did in Scoop's photo—bald oval head and oven mitt hands. Dylan knew instantly those hands would rip him in two.

Dr. Naper looked at it lovingly. "My creation lives."

It was now or never. Dylan snatched up his backpack and ran. "Help! Help!"

He shot through the cemetery, hurdling headstones. "Help!"

He bounded over newly dug graves. "Help!"

His eyes darted left and right, searching the wall. Where's that cratered part? Where?

It finally appeared, barely visible through the haze. Yes!

But just as he reached it, Dr. Naper appeared, blocking it. He wagged a finger at Dylan. "Tsk, tsk. Did you really think I'd let you go?"

Dylan didn't slow. He veered to the right, heading frantically for the gate. *This can't be real! This can't be real!* But real or not, he kept going. *Just breathe. Just breathe and find the gate!*

He dodged trees and stumbled through the gloomy fog. He was so busy panicking, he hadn't realized that something was lurking just behind him. He glanced over his shoulder and—*Ahhhhh!!!*—Naper's monster, Monty, was reaching out for him. "No!"

Dylan bolted away, his sneakers kicking up dirt. But no matter how fast he ran, he could still feel Monty behind him, keeping pace.

"Go away! Go away!"

The gate was just ahead. If he could get out of the graveyard, he'd be safe. Surely the monster couldn't follow. But as he neared it, Dr. Naper appeared again.

"You might as well give up," the ghost said.

"You're insane!" Dylan yelled.

The doctor's face grimaced and his hollow eyes burned red. "No one calls me insane. No one. Ever! Get him, Monty!"

Before Dylan could make another move, the creature's hand gripped his shoulder. It lifted him into the air. "Urrrr," Monty groaned.

"Put me down!" Dylan screamed, kicking and clawing the air. He dangled like an overcooked noodle, suspended from the monster's paw.

The creature lifted Dylan to his nose and sniffed. "Hmmmm . . ."

Uh-oh. "Stop you ugly ape!" Dylan punched Monty hard, his fist connecting with the monster's jaw. But it had all the impact of punching a wall with a marshmallow. It didn't make a mark on Monty. Dylan's hand, however, suffered a raw sting.

Dylan cringed when Monty stuck out his large purple tongue and licked his cheek. Gross!

"Hmmm . . . good."

"Stop!" Dylan cried. "Put me down now."

That's when Monty opened his mouth wide, revealing jagged, green teeth.

Dylan could hear Dr. Naper laughing like a madman.

"You fiend!" Dylan yelled. "Call off your beast!"

"And where is the fun in that?" Dr. Naper said, his voice echoing from a distance.

Dylan fought like crazy, trying to get free of Monty's grip. He was moments away from being a nighttime snack.

That's when a rock the size of a baseball came sailing through the air, whacking the creature right between the eyes.

Monty's face scrunched into a surprised gape. "Huh?" Then another rock flew, hitting the side of his head. "Ow."

Dylan whipped around to see Michael pick up another rock and hurl it at the monster. *Wham!* This one knocked him back.

"Grrrr," the monster groaned, dazed and wobbly. He spun around once, then dropped Dylan from his clutch.

"You came back," Dylan said, shouldering his backpack, ready to scram.

Michael chucked another rock then yelled, "Run!"

Both boys ran for the gate.

But again, Naper stepped in front of it, his eyes lit like fire. "You're going nowhere."

They froze. What now? They couldn't get past him. And how much longer before Monty pulled out of his cloud of confusion?

"You can't keep us here," Michael yelled, throwing a few rocks at Naper. Like with any ghost, the rocks just zipped right through him. They clinked against the iron gate and dropped to the ground. Michael still fired them, one right after the other.

Naper trudged toward them, his eyes glued to Michael.

The rocks were the distraction Dylan needed. He unzipped his backpack, pulled out his camera, and spun around. He held the camera up to Naper's face.

"Say cheese!" Dylan demanded. He snapped the picture, blinding the doctor with the flash.

Naper moaned as he bent over, covering his face with his hands. Dylan and Michael cruised around him, grabbed the harp-shaped gate and flung themselves over. They raced to the bushes, retrieved their bikes, and shot off, away from the graveyard. Dylan didn't catch his breath until they were back at his house.

The boys stood in his front yard, gasping and heaving. "Where'd you run off to?" Dylan asked Michael.

"When Digger showed up, I ran. I was hiding on the other side of the broken wall when I heard you scream."

Dylan nodded, feeling bad. "Sorry I was so rough on you. I guess you weren't a coward after all."

"I couldn't stand by and let that thing rip you apart."

"Thanks." Dylan paused a moment then said, "Guess we won't have that poster after all."

"We won't have that poster," Michael said, "but we can still get old photos and make a montage."

Photos! Dylan looked down at the camera still dangling from the strap on his wrist. "Uh, should we have a look?"

"What do you think is on there?" Michael asked.

"There's only one way to find out." Dylan held his hand steady as he turned the camera on. Instantly, the last photo popped up.

"Holy cheeseburgers!" He'd captured a picture of the evil doctor's face, his mouth a wide O and his eyes bulged with surprise.

They both stared.

"Think we could get an A+ with this?" Michael asked.

Dylan grinned. "I think we have a ghost of a chance."

ENDING 2: DYLAN'S EPITAPH

As Dylan worked furiously, a sharp pain ran up his arm and into his shoulder. He ignored it. *A+...A+...A+...* he kept telling himself.

And why had Michael skipped out? *Wait till I get my hands on that little weasel*, he thought, grinding into the paper.

Doctor Thaddeus Naper

1846 – 1914

Here Lies the Real Monster

He had to have this epitaph. He needed it. It's what drove him to finish.

Finally, he was done. Exhaling a train of shaky breath, he dropped the charcoal and sat back on his heels. After wiping his forehead with his sleeve, he loosened the tape. Then he gently removed the paper. He picked up his flashlight, beat it with the heel of his hand a few times, and—*click!*—it came on.

The grave rubbing was perfect. The best he'd ever done. But wait . . .

Dylan fell onto his bottom. The blood drained from his face. *What is this?* He whipped the flashlight beam to the gravestone, then back to the page. Impossible! The epitaph read:

Dylan Rogers

Born August 16, 2002

Died October 2, 2013

Struck Down So Young

Fear sliced through him. His knees wobbled as he stood. Then reality struck. October 2. That was today!

As fear turned to panic, Dylan gasped and dropped the grave rubbing to the ground. A brisk wind picked it up and blew it against his leg. He screamed, dancing about and hitting at it like someone shaking off a spider.

Then, Dylan ran. He sped through the dark cemetery, dodging trees and jumping headstones. *It's a dream. It's a dream. It's a... nightmare!*

"Michael! Michael! Where are you?" Dylan yelled. He sped on, thinking only of getting out of that graveyard. Just as the front gate came into view, he tripped over a flat grave marker. A burning pain shot though his leg. He rolled over to examine the damage. His jeans were torn; exposing his scraped and bloody knee. But he had to keep moving!

Dylan got up and did a wild hop-limp to the entrance. *Open, please!* But the harp-shaped gate was still locked tight.

"Open!" he shouted, shaking it wildly. Tears stung his eyes. He ran his hand along the stone fence as he hobbled to the spot he'd climbed earlier. With weak and shaky arms, he managed to pull himself over and rush back onto the highway.

He stood staring at the graveyard, trying to make sense of what had just happened. A trick of the light? Yeah, that had to be it. What other explanation could there be?

He wiped sweat from his eyes as he panted like a thirsty dog. That's when a blaring horn snapped him out of his daze. Two bright headlights zoomed toward him with the speed of a runaway train.

Dylan panicked and froze. Then something hit him with such force, it knocked him into the ditch. He looked up at the stars and thought about his epitaph.

Dylan Rogers

August 16, 2002

October 2, 2013

Struck Down So Young

Struck down so young. He tried to flex his fingers. Am I dead?

Then he heard a groan that was not his own. Digger O'Malley was next to him, spitting dirt out of his mouth.

"What's wrong with you, boy?" Digger asked.

"Are you crazy? Standing out in the middle of the road like that! You came close to having your own tombstone."

He stood and brushed himself off. Then he reached a hand down to Dylan and hoisted him to his feet.

"You're lucky I came when I did. Here." Digger tossed Dylan's backpack to the ground. "You forgot this, too." He shoved the grave rubbing toward him.

"No!" Dylan screamed. He tripped to the ground and did a spider crawl, trying to back away.

"Crazy kid," Digger said, pitching the poster. "Stay out of my graveyard!" He turned and hobbled away, back toward the cemetery gate.

Dylan's heart raced as he stared at the paper lying upside down near the road. Maybe it was just a trick of the light.

Dylan crawled toward it. It had to be a trick

of the light. He closed his eyes, held his breath, and flipped it over. Opening one eye, then the other, he looked at the poster. A dim streetlight lit the words.

Doctor Thaddeus Naper

1846 – 1914

Here Lies the Real Monster

Dylan's epitaph had vanished.

* * *

The next afternoon, Michael peeked into Dylan's room. "Uh . . . you weren't at school today."

Dylan sighed. "Yeah, I wasn't feeling good." He couldn't bring himself to tell Michael the truth. That his mind had played a trick on him. One that nearly put him in his own grave. "So what happened to you?"

"I told you I had to use the bathroom. So I snuck around behind the Hanging Tree. That's when I saw that caretaker sneaking up on you. I did what any coward would do. I ran."

Dylan cut him a look. "Thanks a lot. I'll remember that next time you're in trouble."

"Sorry," Michael said. "Did that dude conk you over the head with his shovel?" Michael stopped short and looked around. "Wait. What happened to your room?"

All the epitaph posters were gone, leaving the walls bare and empty. Dylan shrugged, pretending it was no big deal. "I got tired of all the weirdness. It was a stupid hobby anyway."

Panic crossed Michael's face. "I hope you kept the one for Dr. Naper. It's due tomorrow!"

Dylan sauntered over to his closet and took it out. It was rolled up neatly and secured with a rubber band. "Here, you hang on to it."

"Did it come out okay?" Michael asked.

Dylan nodded. "A+."

ENDING 3: SURROUNDED

Dylan continued with the rubbing. His arm kept circling and circling with the charcoal. Just one corner left! It was then that he felt someone looming behind him.

"Michael, where have you been?" he said without stopping.

A woman's voice replied, "Dylan, don't you love us anymore?"

Dylan's heart skipped as he whipped around. Standing over him was something that had once been human. Dylan scrambled back.

"Wh-wh-what?" Dylan stared up at the corpse. "Who are you?"

The dead woman's grinned. "It's me, Harriet. You have my epitaph on your wall."

Dylan freaked. "Y-you're Harriet Honey? But you're dead," he said.

She crossed her bony arms. "Thanks for reminding me."

What's happening? Dylan wondered. *Is this a prank?* "Michael, is that you?"

"Hardly," a voice called from behind him.

Dylan spun around so fast his head swam. A grizzled old corpse with a black mustache and peeling flesh glared at him. He jiggled a toothpick between his teeth. He had a whip looped in his hand. No wait, it was a snake!

Dylan froze. "Theodore Wake?"

"You should know," he said, unwinding the snake. "You did a rubbing of my tombstone."

Dylan ducked. "Ahhhh! Go away!"

Theodore shifted the toothpick from one side of his mouth to the other. "That's what I thought. We ain't important to you anymore."

"I don't know what you mean," Dylan cried.

Before Harriet or Theodore had a chance to answer, Peter Durbin appeared. *Hiccup!* Every time he hiccupped, his powdered wig danced on his head.

"Because of you," he leered at Dylan, "my hiccups are back." *Hiccup!*

"But I didn't ask you to come," Dylan said.

Peter straightened his wig. "I have to know, Dylan." *Hiccup!* "Don't you love us anymore?"

"I don't understand," Dylan sobbed.

"You would trade all our epitaphs for that one," Harriet said. She pointed to the headstone he leaned against.

Just last night he'd said he wanted this epitaph so badly, the others didn't matter anymore. Now, those dearly departed were approaching!

They staggered, moaning and groaning as they circled him.

"Nooooo!" Dylan was surrounded by zombies! "Michael! Digger! Help me!"

"No one's coming," Theodore said. "They've abandoned you. Just like you abandoned us."

"But-but—" Dylan didn't know what to say. He couldn't just stand there and get ripped apart by this herd of decaying creatures. Just as he was ready to bolt, a grubby hand shot up from the grave and gripped his ankle.

"Ahhhh!" Dylan twisted and yanked, trying to break free. Then the skeletal face of Dr. Naper rose up from the dirt—worms slithering in and out of his nose and ears.

"Please don't leave me, Dylan," he pleaded. "You haven't finished the rubbing."

Using his other foot, Dylan stomped down on the Naper's arm. "Let go of me!"

The doctor's hand sprang open and Dylan ran. He barreled across the graveyard, running toward the gate. But the army of the dead were in pursuit, chasing after him.

Dylan didn't look back. He could hear them close behind. *How can dead people be so speedy?* he wondered.

Finally, Dylan reached the gate. But so did the ghosts. They snatched at his jeans and sneakers trying to hold him back. He pushed and kicked until he managed to climb over. After dropping down on the other side, he paused, catching his breath.

"Ha ha!" he laughed, stepping back. "You can't get me now."

But the walking dead are more flexible than he thought. They squeezed through the iron bars like toothpaste squeezed from the tube.

"What? No!" Dylan was on the move again. He hurried to the bushes to find his bike, but Peter grabbed his T-shirt, jerking him back. *Hiccup!*

"Stop!" Dylan yelled. Then, thinking quickly, he snatched Peter's wig from his head.

Peter let go, his eyes wide. "Give that back!"

"No problem." Dylan tossed it behind the bushes, then he dashed off the other way. He ran along the highway, hoping to flag down a car. Not a headlight in sight. "Help!"

The throng of zombies were gaining on him. He picked up speed. But so did they. *Don't you love us anymore?*

Main Street was just ahead. He pumped his arms as his feet flew faster. He scanned all the shops and buildings, hoping to find one open. But they were all dark, locked up tight.

The ghosts were closing in again.

Dylan cut around a corner and across the park. Then he saw it, towering before him. The World's Largest Cheese Grater. His feet pounded the grass as he ran for it.

He jumped onto the side of the grater, shinnying his way up like a monkey on a pole. He drew upward, careful not to slice his hands on the sharp blades.

Finally, Dylan made it. Below, the ghosts stretched their arms upward.

How had he gotten into this fix? All he wanted was that cool poster and an A+.

Suddenly, the grater swayed. The grave-dwellers rattled it as they chanted. Dylan hung on as the grater teetered and tottered, waffling back and forth. It popped and creaked.

And just as the grater tumbled forward, Dylan leaped, hitting and rolling across the grass. He looked up in time to see the grater fall upon the ghosts, mushing them like cottage cheese.

When he reached home, Michael was waiting for him on the front porch. "Where'd you go?" he asked.

"Where'd you go?" Dylan countered.

"When Digger showed up, I ran. I hid behind the caved-in wall, waiting. I finally went back in looking for you. You forgot this." He shoved Dylan's backpack toward him. "And this." He pulled out the grave rubbing.

"I don't want it!"

Michael looked at the poster, then back at Dylan. "Are you kidding me? You put me through all that and now you don't want it? What about our assignment?"

Dylan took the grave rubbing and ripped it in half. "Suddenly Roberta Roberts and her amazing map doesn't seem so boring."

"Whatever," Michael said, hopping on his bike. "See you tomorrow."

Dylan grabbed his backpack and slipped inside. He stood outside his bedroom door a full minute before gathering the nerve to go in.

One by one he ripped the epitaphs off his walls, wadded them up, and took them to the garage.

"Nope," he said, cramming them into the recycling bin. "I don't love you anymore!"

WRITE YOUR OWN ENDING

There were three endings to choose from in *Beyond the Grave*. Did you find the ending you wanted from the story? Did you want something different to happen?

Now it is your turn! Write an ending you would like to happen for Dylan, Michael, and the grave rubbings. Be creative!